Cat & Cat

PAPERCUTZ

MORE GREAT GRAPHIC NOVEL SERIES AVAILABLE FROM
PAPERCUTZ™

THE SMURFS #21

CAT & CAT #1

BARBIE #1

THE SISTERS #1

TROLLS #1

GERONIMO STILTON #17

THEA STILTON #6

THE ONLY LIVING GIRL #1

DINOSAUR EXPLORERS #1

SCARLETT

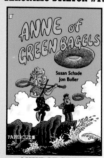
ANNE OF GREEN BAGELS #1

DRACULA MARRIES FRANKENSTEIN!

THE RED SHOES

THE LITTLE MERMAID

FUZZY BASEBALL #1

HOTEL TRANSYLVANIA #1

THE LOUD HOUSE #1

MANOSAURS #1

THE ONLY LIVING BOY #5

GUMBY #1

WWW.PAPERCUTZ.COM
ALSO AVAILABLE WHERE EBOOKS ARE SOLD.

1. GIRL MEETS CAT

CHRISTOPHE CAZENOVE
HERVÉ RICHEZ
SCRIPT

YRGANE RAMON
ART

PAPERCUTZ
New York

To my parents,

To Kali, Patate & Pitou, Toudougras

To Kalysia, Homer, Clovis, Flûte, Hermès…and all the Ronrons!
To Qwertt, Minimia, Chablis, June & Guiness.
To Ricqles, who took good care of Taz, Mitsy, Gimli, and K2000.
To Olivier, Kiwi's official veterinarian in real life, and Sushi's in the comicbook.
To Kiwi, my valiant, affectionate bunny, who waited patiently for me to finish this comicbook
to get out of his cage again.
To Nuggets, Moumoute, Batman, Tweedledee & Tweedledoo, Watson, Chaussette & Mascarpone,
Pompidou, Adolfina, and all the cats abandoned in streets and elsewhere.
To my friends and all those who enjoyed this book.
To my cat. Thanks.
Thanks to SaruJin and Guillaume T. for their help prepping for setting the color when finishing the book.
http://www.yrgane.com
– Yrgane

For Céline, who loved doing the butterfly and who'll love not doing it anymore…
– Hervé

Cat & Cat

#1 "Girl Meets Cat"
Christophe Cazenove &
Hervé Richez – Writers
Yrgane Ramon – Artist
Joe Johnson – Translator
Wilson Ramos Jr. – Letterer

Special thanks to Catherine Loiselet

Production – Mark McNabb
Managing Editor – Jeff Whitman
Editorial Intern – Izzy Boyce-Blanchard
Jim Salicrup
Editor-in-Chief

© 2012-2020 Bamboo Édition.
All other material © 2020 Papercutz.

Papercutz books may be purchased for business or promotional use. For information on bulk purchases
please contact Macmillan Corporate and Premium Sales Department at (800) 221-795 x5442.

Hardcover ISBN: 978-1-5458-0427-8
Paperback ISBN: 978-1-5458-0428-5

Printed in China
February 2020

Distributed by Macmillan
First Papercutz Printing

When you have a cat, you have to fight for its rights. Because cats are born free just like you and me...

But DAD, why won't you let him GO OUT?!

This is my final decision. It's too dangerous outside for an apartment cat.

÷Pffff÷ Whatever. For starters, we live in a house!

Same thing. When you get a cat, he's gotta stay shut inside for at least a week...

The house needs to pick up his scent for it to become his territory...

Blah blah blah!

...Otherwise he'll never find his way back home the first time he goes out!

You're locking him up when he's basically 21 in human years. I really need to fight to let him out of here.

Pout all you like, I'm IN-FLE-XI-BLE!

MEEEEEOoOOOOOOooWWW!

SCHING   SCHING   SCHING   SCHING

My cat is more equal than others!

8

I'd like to be an astronaut cat!

If nothing else, just to munch my dry food while weightless, ha ha!

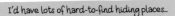

I'd have lots of hard-to-find hiding places...

No, Sushi, not in my helmet!

Tons of games to play...

I've got to have THAT ball!

My master would install a cat door just for me...

Oops!

It's like he's afraid of the cat door...

Your cat is sooo weird!

You're going into that carrier, doggone it!

If you say "doggone it," it's not surprising that he's afraid. Dogs stress him out!

We bought him an extra-large version JUST so he wouldn't be stressed!

BOING

That carrier's practically an apartment!

Okay time to move in, cat!

TAP TAP

Come on, Sushi, cheer up...We're going on vacation!

MMEOW MEEOOOWW... MEOOW

Wait! I have an idea!

Sushi!

Sushi!

PSHEE PSHEE

Come on, Sushi!

RING RING RING

Easy peasy! Who has the best ideas, huh?

Well done, Cat...

This is by far the most stress-free solution for everybody!

Hey!

SQUEE SQUEE SQUEE

20

People saying that cats have nine lives is no joke!

I ought to know...

BOOOM

The first time, I stupidly bit the dust while crossing the street...

BOOOM

SPLOTCH

...and back then, they didn't care about right-of-way!

BOOM BOOM BOOM

The second time was in Egypt...

This is all very fancy but they forgot my cat food...

...Locked up with my master the Pharaoh.

Meow!?

I lost my third life during the Hundred Years War...

Charge!

I ran out of luck on the last day of the hundredth year, just before the truce!

Run!

ZOOOOM

Maybe he can read thoughts...

Or simply read!

Or he knows when the telephone's going to ring...

MEOW

Maybe he can foresee catastrophes...

He sees things others don't.

He communicates with cats on other planets!

What are you drawing, CAT?

I'm figuring out what Sushi's sixth sense might be...

What do you think it is?

We'd have to make sure he had the five normal ones first.

Okay, now that it's the weekend, road trip time!

Since the resort we're going to doesn't allow cats, let's go over what you did to make sure Sushi would be happy staying at home...

Oh, uh yes...I fixed him...

...Extra water, which ought to be enough...

I opened three bags of dry food...

...and I piled his dish high!

CHOMPACHAMOMP

CAT CHOMP

I put out some of our clothes, so he'd still have our smell around...

I didn't forget to change his litter box, either!

And lastly, I left a window open wide so he could go for a walk in the yard.

YOU DID WHAT?

Is our weekend road trip over already?

Vvvoooouumm

28

HOW CATS WORK "MEOWING"

MEEOOOOOWWWWW!

I know that one! An empty food dish means an empty belly!

MEEOOOOOWWWW!

That cat wants to go out...

MEWWW!

That cat wants to come back in...

MEOWWW!

A crazy fifteen minutes or so...

MEEOOWW! *MEOWW!* *MEOWW!* *MEOW!* *MEOWWW!* SCRATCH SCRATCH

In urgent need of petting...

RRRWWOOOEM RRRRRR RRRRRRRRR

That's a lot already!

So... meow... meoww... meoww...

Tap Tap Tap

MAHOOWWW!

What? That's a new one...

That's funny! Sushi has decided to study Dad's different screams....

MAHOOOoWWWWW!

Sometimes, I feel like my cat dreams of being an explorer...

But he'd be the kind of explorer to leave without food...

SHOOFFF

MEOW!

Because Sushi doesn't want to explore just anywhere. Really...

MEOW!

WHEEEEEEEE,

Really, he'd just love to explore the land of the "cold food box"...

So let's not bother him!

Cat, let me get to the spinach, we need to eat!

Never!

BADA BOOM

Ha ha! What a fraidy-cat!

It's just a huuuuuge storm, Sushi...nothing to be scared of!

Not here...

Not here either...

Sushi?

Hey...What's that I see snuggled under my sweaters?

CAT! You'll never guess where that fraidy-cat went to hide!

HAHAHA

Uh, yes, I will!

Is the storm over yet?

44

Okay, SUSHI. Stop it, please.

Aren't you kind of lax with your cat?

Kind of what?

You're too nice. With a cat you must be very firm.

MUNCH CHOMP CRUNCH

Don't hesitate to punish him.

Without beating him, obviously.

You must put his nose in his mess and give him a little pop on his butt.

BOING
PLIP
PLOP

When you catch him in the act, a little squirt of water at that very instant or in the next five seconds.

POW BOOM ZAP

But the most important of all is putting a finger on his nose while saying firmly "NO! NO!"

Will you get mad if I don't follow your advice right away?

In a house, when you have a cat, you must think about its freedom.

MEEEOOWWW

Come in...

That's why Dad decided to install a cat door.

Unfortunately, our cat door squeaks.

SQUEEEE

And at night, a cat goes in and out every four minutes or so...

SQUEEEE

SQUEEEE

SQUEEEE

SQUEEE

SQUEE

...a cat door gets stuck sometimes, too.

MEEEOOOWWW

Meow

Meeeow

oo ooOwww

And once you get it unstuck...

...you'd better have put away all your papers.

Z

CRAK

That's why Dad put a lock on the cat door.

MEEEOOW?!

wooee
wrooeee
wv
voOooooee
wee

Because in a house, when you have a cat, you also need to think about YOUR freedom.

HURRY, DADDY! His stomach's really hurting!

VETERINARY CLINIC

VET MOBILE

MEOUCH
MEOUCH

WOOF

Hmm...we'll do an X-ray!

POKE

MMOOOWW

Okay, come this way a bit and don't move!

X-RAY

MEEEOOWWW

This tummy ache comes from your cat loving mice too much.

?!

No way! He's SO clumsy he never catches any!

Also my kitty REALLY doesn't like to run!

It's not his thing.

I had to put out mousetraps everywhere. Ironic when you have a tomcat in the house!

Then, I'll confirm what I said...especially now that I've seen the X-ray.

Your cat loves mice too much...

And, I see, he doesn't need to run to get them...

63

Sometimes, I call my cat a pirate...

Because I really believe he thinks he's CAPTAIN CAT SPARROW, the terror of the 7 seas.

POW
POW

BOOM

BLACK CAT

CATNIP'S REVENGE!

I can picture him leading a mutiny...

...Leaping into the air to go plunder an enemy ship.

Continuously slashing at the enemy captain with great blows...

...Chasing him from atop the foremast...

....Leaping in pursuit of him, his claws planted in the sail.

SCCRRRRRYYYYY

It's well known that pirates live by their own code!

Get over it, Dad. They're just curtains...

I always pay careful attention not to disturb my Sushi!

SQUEAK

ZZRRRRRR

TIPPY TAP

SNORE

ZZZZZZZ

⧽GAG!⧽

eeerrk

He's my kitty-cat, I ought to respect his sleep!

I just wish he'd do the same with me...

SNORFF

ZZZZZZZZ

Sushi has an AWESOME sense of smell!

SNIF SNIF SNIF

At every meal, he hurtles in like a madman, especially on Mondays when Dad makes salmon!

SHWEEFF

On Tuesdays, it's burgers, and he's there first!

MEOWWWW

On Wednesdays, stuffed tomatoes and Zwoop! There's Sushi!

SNNUUUURffff

On Thursdays, he NEVER misses out on roasted pork!

MMMM YMMM

Sushi arrives even faster on Fridays for ravioli.

Dad only tries out new recipes on Saturdays.

Come on, Cat, time to eat!

KRR KRR KRR

Hey...Sushi isn't here. Do you think he's sick?

His sniffer must be broken!

What were you saying about Sushi's sniffer?

NEW NUGGETS

SUPER SUNDAE

PUSH

All right, already... I won't invent new recipes on Saturdays.

I wonder where Sushi is...

If you want to find him, you just have to get him to come!

How?

Okay, Gladys, it's easy-peasy! A cat is CONDITIONED! I'll show you with my very own Sushi!

You open the refrigerator door and... ABRACADABRA!

There he is! CONDITIONED, I'm telling you!

MIEEEwww

Wow, incredible! It's so easy doing what you want with a cat!

District College Mysteries!

We almost missed the new episode!

ZOOOMMAZZOOOOM

District College and... ABRACADABRA!

What are you doing, Cat?

I'm making a scary costume...

BOOOOOOO

That's fun... For Halloween?

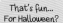

No, to get Sushi to come inside! Hey help me slip into my costume!

Dad told me not to try to catch him but to scare him instead...

Otherwise, it's impossible to get him to come in the house...

I understand!

Okay. Here goes!

CATMAGGEDON!

But, Dad...Why are you keeping Sushi from coming in?!

HEEHEEHEE

Plop

CLAK CLAK CLAK CLAK CLAK CLAK CLAK CLAK CLAK

MEEEEOOW

Heehee, I'd really like to be a Ghost Cat in a haunted house!

BOOOOOOOO BOOOOOOOO

I'd go through walls just like this!

To scare visitors...

AAAHH!

...to chase mice...

BOOOO!

EEEK!

...or drive all the doggies mad!

HEE HEE HEE

This is the life!

SNIP

BONK

Dad, I think Sushi wants us to put cat-beds on the walls, too...

KRACK
KRACK

What if we adopted a normal cat instead?

79

That's an awesome surprise you're making for your dad's birthday, Cat!

Yep!

Yes, a tee-shirt decorated with a portrait of his adored daughter...

Such a good likeness!

With my lovable Sushi on the back!

HEEHEE

I hope he doesn't come home before you're done!

No worries!

I put a bell on Sushi's collar!

?

And? What's that got to do with it?

Well, see...That way, I always know where my kitty is!

DILING
DILING
DILING
DILING
DILING

There, he's in the yard...

DILING
DILING
DILING

You hear him?

...and he's heading towards the garage!

DILING
DILING
DILING

So, I know where Dad is, TOO!

In the yard, by the garage...

SUSHI! DILING
GET OUT OF MY ROSEBEDS!
DILING
:RHAAAH!:
LET GO OF THAT WATERING HOSE!
DILING DILING

≯Argh!≮ Why did you show him that?! There's no using the printer without that hysterical monster hurtling in!

You should try to set a good example for him instead!

Bill Reminder!

Because that's a good example, yeah?

Dad, Gladys is coming over with Avalanche! She's going to introduce him to Sushi!

Avalanche?

Yes, he's a brand new, all-white cat! She could have named him Snow, but Avalanche fits his personality more, seeing as how he breaks everything in his wake! A real cyclone!

Whoa, whoa, whoa, young lady!

Do you know when you bring an animal in a house where one already lives, it's better to introduce them outside?

Oh, no, why?

Because if Sushi sees another cat coming into his home, he'll want to defend his territory, and they'll end up fighting!

ROOAR
SCRATCH
SCRATCH
SCRATCH

Hmm....What you're saying makes sense...

Hello, Cat Girl!

?!

Come into the yard, Gladys! It's the best place for Avalanche to meet Sushi!

Why's that?

A matter of territory, fighting, I don't know what else...

It's not because my cat is named Avalanche, is it?

ZWIPP

FRUSH

ZWIPP

PLOP

MEEOWWW

MEEOWW

MEOOOW

MEEOW   MEOOW

I think I'm going to widen the cat door. It must be too little for him...

Yeah, it's clear he's not going through there!

WATCH OUT FOR PAPERCUTZ™

Welcome to the first feline & family-friendly CAT & CAT graphic novel, by Christophe Cazenove & Hervé Richez, writers, and Yrgane Ramon, artist, from Papercutz, those animal-lovers dedicated to publishing great graphic novels for all ages. I'm Jim Salicrup, the Editor-in-Chief and litter-box-cleaner, here to talk about cats. Seems that there are so many cats featured in our graphic novels, that it's often suggested that we change our name to *Papercatz*. Obviously, we must love cats, with CAT & CAT simply being the latest addition to our feline line-up. Here's a list of some of the other cats you'll find at Papercutz...

Azrael – This naughty kitty belongs to the Smurfs's archfoe, Gargamel. Azrael would love nothing better than to eat a Smurf! You can find Azrael in THE SMURFS graphic novels by Peyo (writer/artist).

Brina – A two-year-old city cat, named Brina, takes a summer vacation in the country with her owners. Here she meets a group of stray cats who call themselves "The Gang of the Feline Sun," who convince her to runaway with them and live life as a free cat. While Brina enjoys her newfound freedom, her young owners are distraught over losing her, someone they consider a member of their family. Brina is terribly conflicted and must choose to return to her owners or to continue to live free in the wild. Find out more in the preview, by Georgio Salati, writer and Christian Cornia, artist, on the next page.

Cartoon – Is a pretty happy cat, and he lives with Chloe and her family. CHLOE, by Greg Tessier (writer) and Amandine (artist) is published by Charmz, a Papercutz imprint focused on young love. Even though Cartoon is a minor character in CHLOE, he's proven so popular that he'll soon have a graphic novel of his very own: CHLOE & CARTOON!

Cliff – Is the pet cat of the Loud family and is just one of the many occupants of THE LOUD HOUSE. There's Lincoln Loud, his ten sisters (Lori, Leni, Luna, Luan, Lynn, Lucy, Lisa, Lola, Lana, and Lily), his parents (Rita and Lynn Sr.), and the other pets, Charles (a dog), El Diablo (a snake), Hops (a frog), Walt (a bird), and Geo (a hamster). Cliff may not be the star of THE LOUD HOUSE, but the fact is that the Nickelodeon animated series is a big hit, as are the Papercutz graphic novels, so who's to say he's not a part of what's making THE LOUD HOUSE so successful?

Hubble – Is the snarky pet cat of the Monroe family, and the unofficial mascot of the GEEKY F@B 5. Hubble has watched sisters Lucy and Marina Monroe, start up the Geeky F@b 5 with their friends, Zara, A.J., and Sofia, and tackle all sorts of problems, including finding homes for pets when the local animal shelter suffers major damage from a tornado. Even Hubble must admit that when girls stick together, anything is possible! Written by mother/daughter writing team, Liz & Lucy Lareau, and drawn by artist Ryan Jampole.

Pussycat -- Before Peyo created THE SMURFS he wrote and drew the adventures of PUSSYCAT. Pussycat is a lovable, mischievous tuxedo cat who spends his time chasing after milk and snacks and framing other members of his family for his shenanigans Warning: our hero Pussycat is a real cat. He does not speak (he just meows) and his main passions in life are eating, hunting mice, avoiding dogs, and meowing at night. All of Pussycat's adventures were collected in one deluxe volume entitled, PUSSYCAT.

Scarlett – Scarlett, as revealed in SCARLETT "Star on the Run" by Jon Buller (author/artist) and Susan Schade (author/artist), is a small, harlequin-colored cat and a huge movie star. And what's more — she talks! Unfortunately she's also abused by her producer, so she dreams of only one thing: escaping! When the occasion presents itself, she runs for her life.

Sybil – Is the cute cat owned by fourteen-year-old (soon to be fifteen) Amy Von Brandt. Amy's life is never dull, and you can find out all about her and Sybil in AMY'S DIARY by Véronique Grisseaux (writer) and Laëtitia Ayné(artist), based on the novels by India Desjardins, and published by Charmz.

We could go on and on, but we think you get the point! (We didn't even mention Geronimo Stilton's purr-sistant foes, the Pirate Cats, who in the GERONIMO STILTON graphic novels, are always trying to rewrite history to their advantage!) Instead, we'll just ask you to keep an eye out for the next CAT & CAT graphic novel, and to watch out for Papercutz!

Thanks,

Jim

STAY IN TOUCH!

EMAIL: salicrup@papercutz.com
WEB: www.papercutz.com
TWITTER: @papercutzgn
INSTAGRAM: @papercutzgn
FACEBOOK: PAPERCUTZGRAPHICNOVELS
FANMAIL: Papercutz, 160 Broadway, Suite 700, East Wing, New York, NY 10038

The Gang of the Feline Sun #1

Warm sun and fresh air, with a hint of fir trees. Something totally new for Brina.

I'VE NEVER BEEN HERE BEFORE.

It's the mountains.

AAAHH!

FINALLY... VACATION.

AND FREEDOM.

©2020 TUNUÉ (Tunué s.r.l.) – Giorgio Salati and Christian Cornia

Find your way to wherever fine books are sold and pick up **BRINA** the **CAT**

The Gang of the Feline Sun #1